M·USE'S
FIRST SPRING

Lauren Thompson

ILLUSTRATED BY
Buket Erdogan

Simon & Schuster Books for Young Readers

New York   London   Toronto   Sydney

To Katie and Nicky—L. T.

To my dear sister Emnos,
for all our differences and your sweet friendship;
and to a dear friend, Linda,
for your wisdom and support.
Thank you—B. E.

SIMON & SCHUSTER BOOKS FOR YOUNG READERS
An imprint of Simon & Schuster Children's Publishing Division
1230 Avenue of the Americas, New York, New York 10020
Text copyright © 2005 by Lauren Thompson
Illustrations copyright © 2005 by Buket Erdogan
SIMON & SCHUSTER BOOKS FOR YOUNG READERS is a
trademark of Simon & Schuster, Inc.
Book design by Mark Siegel
Manufactured in China
10 9 8 7 6 5 4 3 2 1
Library of Congress Cataloging-in-Publication Data
Thompson, Lauren.
Mouse's first spring / Lauren Thompson ; illustrated by Buket
Erdogan.— 1st ed.
p. cm.
Summary: A mouse and its mother experience the delights of
nature on a windy spring day.
ISBN 0-689-85838-8
[1. Nature—Fiction. 2. Winds—Fiction. 3. Spring—Fiction.
4. Mother and child—Fiction. 5. Mice—Fiction.] I. Erdogan,
Buket, ill. II. Title.
PZ7.T37163Mo 2005
[E]—dc22   2004014501

first
edition

One windy spring day,
Mouse and
Momma went
out to play!

There in the grass,
Mouse found something
glittery and *flittery*.
What can it be? wondered
Mouse.

"Look!" said Momma.
"A butterfly!"

Then *whoosh!* blew the wind, and *fluttery buttery* the butterfly flew away.

There under a leaf,
Mouse found something
slithery and slimy.

What can it be?
wondered
Mouse.

"Look!" said Momma.
"A snail!"

Then *whoosh!* blew the wind, and *hidey insidey* the snail hid away.

There on a branch,
Mouse found something

feathery

and plump.

What can it be?
wondered Mouse.

"Look!" said Momma. "A bird!"

Then *whoosh!* blew the wind, and *dip flip flap* the bird darted away.

There by the pond,
Mouse found
something
green
and peeping.

What can it be?
wondered Mouse.

"Look!" said Momma.
"A frog!"

Then *whoosh!* blew
the wind, and

splishy splash

the frog hopped

away.

There in the dirt,
Mouse found something
pink and wiggly.

What can it be?
wondered Mouse.

"Look!" said Momma. "A worm!"

Then *whoosh!* blew the wind, and

squiggly squeeze
the worm slid away.

There on a stem,
Mouse found
something
sweet and petally.

What can it be? wondered Mouse.

"Look!" said Momma. "A flower!"

Then *whoosh!* blew the wind, and *rumply bumply* Mouse tumbled away!

Then all
around, Mouse
felt something
soft and cuddly,
and oh-so-cozy.

What can it be?
wondered Mouse.

Smooch!
came a kiss

and *oooch!*
came a hug!

"It's me!" said Momma.

"Spring is here, little Mouse,
and I love you!"